AUTHOR'S NOTE

Pinocchio is one of the most fascinating characters in all of children's literature: sassy, naughty, thoughtless, and certainly irresponsible, yet amazingly endearing. Perhaps he is so loved because he is all of us: in the beginning mere chunks of wood, upon which the carver Experience creates a whole human being. Perhaps he is so loved because he is so outrageous, such a brilliant mirror of human nature. Certainly he is theatrical.

The Adventures of Pinocchio explodes into brilliant, good-humored repartee, unforgettable slapstick, and exaggerated adventure—all stocks in trade of the Italian traveling theater, the *commedia dell' arte*. Even one of the *commedia's* stock characters, Harlequin, makes it into the book, in the Fire-eater scene.

Undoubtedly seeing a glimpse of themselves, audiences of this seventeenth- and eighteenth-century theater loved the vulnerability of the *commedia* characters: the naiveté of Harlequin, the greed of Pantaloon, the flirtatiousness of Columbine, the guile of Scaramouche. Collodi (Carlo Lorenzini), a journalist, born in Florence in 1826 when the *commedia* was so popular, embraces that human vulnerability in his book. Each character mirrors some aspect of Pinocchio himself: Fox and Cat, his greed; Fire-eater, his vulnerability to authority; the Blue Fairy, his sensitivity to the mother figure; Candlewick, his unbridled spirit.

At the same time, Pinocchio mirrors us. We are Pinocchio. And the characters are us. What better place for us to face ourselves than in story, and theater?

It is for this reason that I have chosen to celebrate the enchanting story of Pinocchio in scenes that will, I hope, encourage readers of every age to come to the stage. To read *Pinocchio*. And to stage *Pinocchio*. You will be part of a long and old and wonderful tradition.

ADAPTATION FROM

C. COLLODI'S

Pinocchio

ED YOUNG

PHILOMEL BOOKS · NEW YORK

Adapted from the original version of *The Adventures of Pinocchio*, translated by
M.A. Murray and published in the United Kingdom by Unwin in 1892.

Patricia Lee Gauch, Editor.

Jacket lettering by John Stevens. Title page lettering by Gunta Alexander.
Library of Congress Cataloging-in-Publication Data
Collodi, Carlo, 1826-1890. [Avventure di Pinocchio. English]
Pinocchio / C. Collodi : illustrated by Ed Young; adapted from
M.A. Murray's translation of C. Collodi's story. p. cm.
Summary: The adventures of a talking wooden puppet whose nose
grows whenever he tells a lie. [1. Fairy tales. 2. Puppets—Fiction.]
I. Young, Ed, ill. II. Title. PZ8.C7Ph 1996
[Fic]—dc20 95-10127 CIP AC
ISBN 0-399-22941-8
1 3 5 7 9 10 8 6 4 2
First Impression

To
Patricia Gauch,
by whose light
this block of
Aspen wood
took voice
and form.

—E.Y.

SCENE I
Master Cherry's story

THERE WAS ONCE UPON A TIME an extraordinary piece of wood. I should know: I found it in my shop and thought it would make a splendid leg of a little table. But when I took my ax to it, I heard a small voice. "Do not strike me so hard," it said.

"Where on earth can that little voice have come from?" I said to myself. I decided it was purely my imagination, and began to polish the piece of wood when the same little voice said, "Stop! You're tickling me." Can you imagine my astonishment!

At that moment someone knocked at my door. It was old Geppetto, a lively old fellow whom all the neighborhood boys called Polendina, corn pudding, because that is what his yellow wig looked like.

"I'd like to make a beautiful wooden puppet," he said to me. "One that can dance and fence and leap like an acrobat. I could travel the world over with it and earn a pretty penny," he said. "What do you think?"

"Fine idea, Polendina," I said.

"Polendina!" he said. "Polendina!" he blustered. "Polendina!" he exploded.

He was so enraged that I gave him my piece of wood to make his puppet, but as I handed him the wood, it began to wriggle. Indeed, it wriggled so hard it knocked poor Geppetto in the shins.

"You hit me," Geppetto said.

"The wood hit you."

"You hit me with the wood."

"I did not."

"Liar."

"Polendina!"

"Fool."

"Polendina!"

"Donkey."

"Polendina!"

"Baboon!"

"Polendina! Polendina!"

At that we fell to fighting! But the fight squared the account. Finally we shook hands and Geppetto carried off his fine piece of wood.

. . .

Gᴇᴘᴘᴇᴛᴛᴏ ʟɪᴠᴇᴅ all alone in a single room with an old chair and a broken-down table, but he had a fireplace. When he got home, he lit the fire, took his tools, and began to model his puppet.

"What name shall I give him?" he said to himself. "I think I will call him Pinocchio. I once knew a whole family to be called Pinocchio: Pinocchio the father, Pinocchio the mother, and Pinocchio the children. All of them did well."

Now that the puppet had a name, the old man began to carve, first the hair, then the forehead, and then the eyes. But he had barely finished the eyes, when they moved!

"Wicked wooden eyes," he said. "Why do you look at me?"

Since no one or nothing answered, he carved the nose, but no sooner had he made it than it began to grow. It grew, and grew and grew! Poor Geppetto. The more he cut the nose, the more it grew.

And he had not even finished cutting the mouth when it began to laugh.

"Stop laughing," Geppetto said, but it did not.

"Stop laughing, I say!" Geppetto roared, and it stopped laughing, but stuck out its tongue.

This time Geppetto ignored it and went on carving the chin, the throat, the shoulders, the stomach, the arms, and the hands. That was when the puppet grabbed old Geppetto's wig!

"Oh," said Geppetto, "you are not even finished and you have no respect! You are a bad boy, very bad. Very, very bad."

Even so, Geppetto went on carving the puppet's legs and his feet, and tried to help the little puppet walk. But as soon as his legs were flexible, Pinocchio began to walk by himself, then to run about the room. Finally he ran right out of the door, jumped into the street, and escaped.

"Stop him!" Geppetto shouted. But the people, seeing a puppet racing down the street like a racehorse, laughed and laughed and laughed.

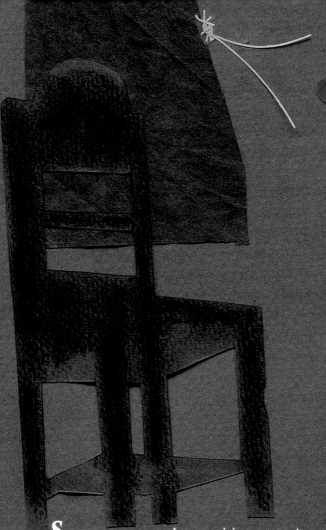

SCENE II

SOME STORIES take surprising turns. A carabineer— that is a policeman—caught the puppet and handed him over to Geppetto. But Pinocchio threw himself on the ground, and when old Geppetto tried to pick him up, people thought that he was beating the puppet.

What did the carabineer do? He led Geppetto off to prison!

"It serves me right," wailed poor Geppetto. "It serves me right."

Did that imp Pinocchio care? No. Finding himself free, he ran off as fast as his legs could carry him. He rushed across fields, jumped high banks, scaled thorny hedges and ditches full of water.

Finally home, he pushed the door open and threw himself on the ground, giving a great sigh. That was when he heard something or someone say:

"Cricri-cri!"

"Who is calling me?"

"It's me," said a big Cricket.

"I live here now," said Pinocchio. "Get along with you."

"Sorry, I can't go. I have a great truth to tell."

"Oh, all right, but be quick about it."

"Woe to children who rebel against their parents and run away from home."

"Sing on, Cricket! I have decided to do just that. Otherwise I shall be sent to school. I'd rather run after butterflies, or climb trees."

"Poor little goose," the Cricket said. "You will grow up a perfect donkey of a boy! Just a wooden head!"

At that Pinocchio jumped up, and snatching a wooden hammer from the bench, he threw it at the Talking Cricket. Splat.

10

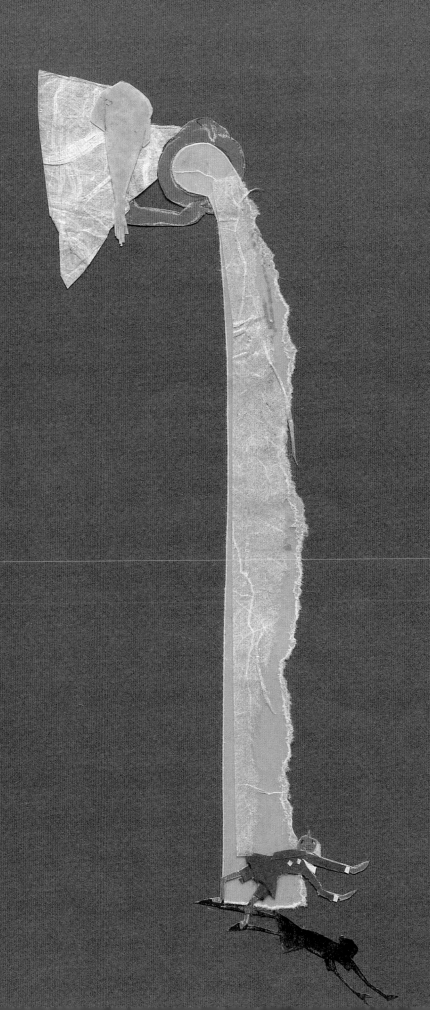

. . .

Now, the shop was still, but night was coming on, and Pinocchio was hungry. He searched drawers, hoping to find a crumb, a crust, a bone left by a dog. He found absolutely nothing. Perhaps, he thought, someone in the neighborhood has a crumb for poor Pinocchio.

And so he went out into a wild and stormy winter's night. A bitter wind whistled angrily, and trees creaked and groaned. But running from house to house, he found the village all dark and deserted. Shops closed, windows shut. Not so much as a dog in the street.

When at last he saw a bell to pull, he pulled it. A man in a nightcap came to a window.

"What do you want at such an hour?" he shouted.

"Would you be kind enough to give me a little bread?"

"Hold out your cap!" the old man said.

Pinocchio had no cap, but he stood under the window. An enormous basin of water poured down on him, watering him from head to foot as if he were a pot of geraniums.

He returned home like a wet chicken, and fell asleep with his feet by the fire, and didn't wake up until he heard someone knocking at the door.

"Who is there?" he said.

"Geppetto," the voice answered.

When Pinocchio hopped up, he discovered his feet had been burned off by the fire!

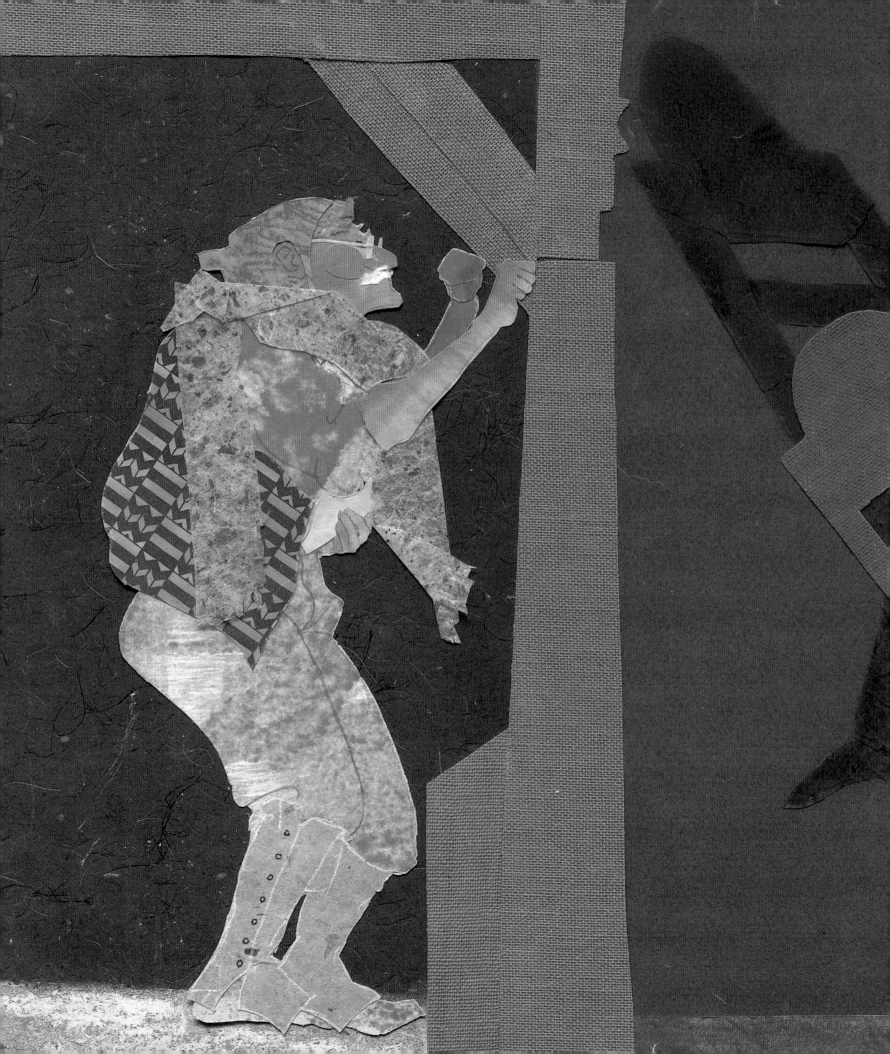

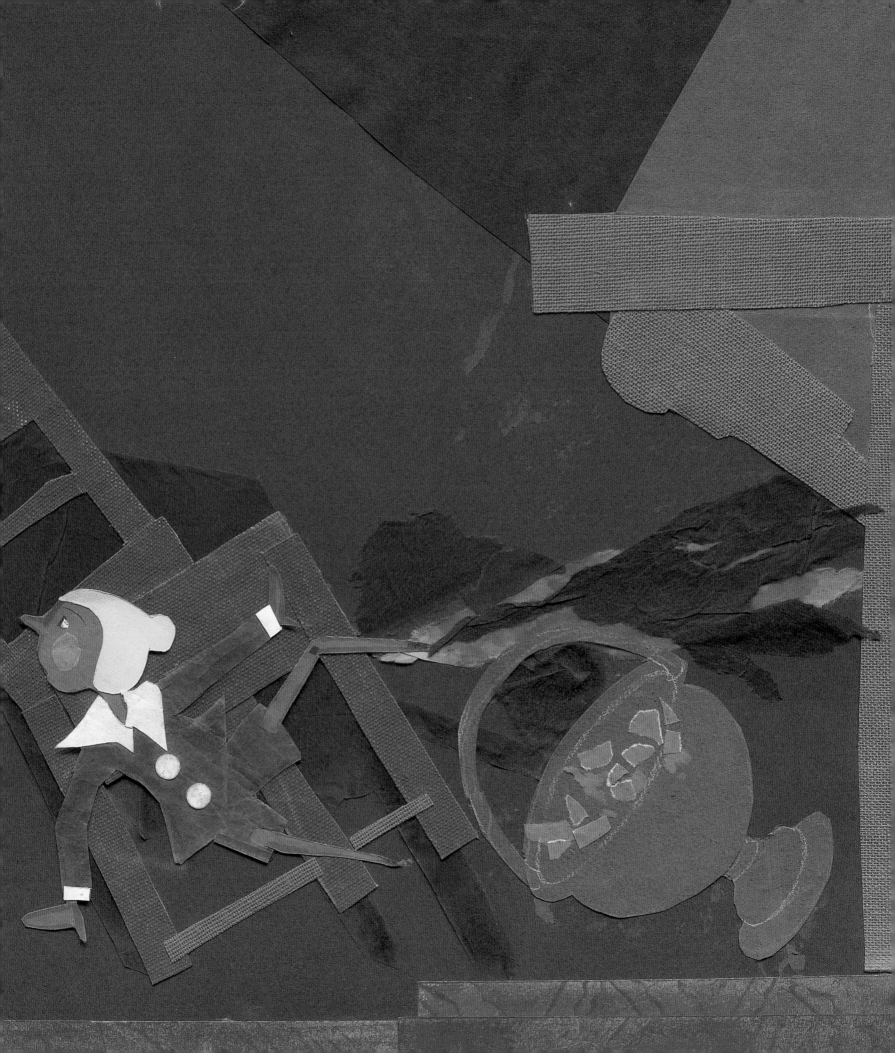

SCENE III

Lᴜᴄᴋʏ ꜰᴏʀ Pɪɴᴏᴄᴄʜɪᴏ, Geppetto, though he put on a stern face, had a heart as big as his own warm room. Without saying a word, he took his tools in hand and in less than an hour, he had made two little feet: swift and well knit.

Pinocchio jumped down from the table and began to spring around the room.

"I am so happy," he said, springing, "that I shall go to school after all."

"Good boy," Geppetto said.

"But I shall need some clothes."

Geppetto, a poor man, made him a little jacket of flowered paper, a pair of shoes from the bark of a tree, and a cap of some crumbs of bread.

"I look quite the gentleman," Pinocchio said, strutting about like a peacock. "But, Papa, I am without the thing I need most."

"What is it?" Geppetto said.

"A spelling book."

"And I have no money to buy one."

Pinocchio became very, very sad.

"Well," exclaimed Geppetto, "patience." Rising, he put on his old, patched red coat and ran out of the house. When he returned, he held in his hand a spelling book. But his coat was gone.

"Papa, your coat," said Pinocchio.

"I have sold it," the old man said.

"Why, Papa?" Pinocchio asked.

"Because . . . because . . . because I found it too hot."

Pinocchio knew better, and sprang up. He threw his arms around Geppetto and began to kiss him again and again.

Tʜᴇ ɴᴇxᴛ ᴅᴀʏ, as soon as it stopped snowing, Pinocchio set out for school with his fine spelling book under his arm. He began talking to himself:

"Today I will begin to read; then tomorrow I will learn to write, and the day after tomorrow I will learn to add and subtract and multiply. Then on the next day, knowing all this, I will earn a great deal of money and buy a beautiful new cloth coat for Papa.

"No, not cloth. It shall be made all of gold and silver, and it shall have diamond buttons."

While he was earnestly muttering to himself, he thought that he heard music in the distance: *fi-fi-fi, fi-fi-fi, zum, zum zum zum.*

He stopped and listened at a cross street that led to a little village on the seashore. Drums and fifes! Should he go to school? Or should he go after the drums and fifes? Hmmm. He thought.

He shrugged his shoulders. "Today I will go and hear the fifes. Tomorrow I will go to school."

And off he ran. *Fi-fi-fi, zum, zum zum zum.* At last he found himself in the village square, where everyone was crowding around a wooden building, painted a thousand wonderful colors.

"What does it say?" Pinocchio asked, turning to a little boy and pointing to a sign with letters red as fire. "I would read it, but I don't know how."

"What a blockhead! The sign says 'Great Marionette Show Today.' "

"Oh, I must go," said Pinocchio. "How much is it?"

"Twopence."

"Twopence! . . . Would you lend me twopence till tomorrow?"

"Tomorrow, yes, but not today," the boy said.

Pinocchio was frantic. "Will you take my jacket for twopence?" the puppet asked.

"What could I do with a jacket of flowered paper? If there were rain and it got wet, it would be impossible to get it off!"

"Will you buy my shoes?"

"For what? To light the fire?"

"Then how about my cap?"

"A cap of bread crumbs! A mouse would nibble it off my head."

What a crisis! Pinocchio hesitated.

"Will you give me twopence for this new spelling book?"

At that a ragpicker who was listening nearby interrupted.

"I will buy the spelling book for twopence."

And the book was sold there and then, even as poor Geppetto sat in his shirtsleeves at his fire.

SCENE V

THAT NIGHT when Pinocchio told Fire-eater that his father sold his only coat to buy him a spelling book, Fire-eater said: "Poor man! Here are five gold pieces. Go home at once and take them to him with my compliments."

Pinocchio said thank you a thousand times to the showman, and goodbye to every puppet one by one, then set out for home.

But he had not gone far down the lane when he met a Fox lame of one foot and a Cat blind of both eyes, helping each other along.

"Good day, Pinocchio," said the Fox, politely.

"How do you know my name?" asked the puppet.

"I know you and your father well. Only yesterday I saw him at the door of his house."

"Oh, dear Papa. What was he doing?"

"Shivering, in his shirtsleeves."

"Oh, poor Papa. But that is over. He shall shiver no more!"

"Why?" asked the Fox, inching closer to Pinocchio.

"Because I have become a gentleman," said Pinocchio.

Both the Fox and the Cat began to laugh.

"There is nothing to laugh at," said Pinocchio. "You can see by these five gold pieces that I am a gentleman."

At the sympathetic ring of the money, the Fox stretched out the paw that was crippled, and the Cat opened wide her two green eyes.

"And now," whispered the Fox, "what will you do with the money?"

"I will buy a new coat for my papa, made of gold and silver and with diamond buttons. Then I will buy a spelling book for myself."

"For yourself?"

"Yes indeed: for I wish to go to school to study."

"Look at me!" wailed the Fox. "Through my foolish passion for study I have lost a leg."

"Look at me!" whined the Cat. "Through my foolish passion for study I have lost my sight."

"Instead, how would you like to double your money?" asked the Fox.

"Yes indeed," answered Pinocchio, "but how?"

"Come with us to the Land of the Owls."

Pinocchio reflected. "No, I will return to my papa, who is waiting for me."

20

"In the Land of the Owls," said the Fox, "there is a Field of Miracles. Dig a little hole in this field and put in one gold piece, cover it and water it with two pails of water, sprinkle two pinches of salt, and in the night it will grow and flower. Soon you will find a beautiful tree laden with gold coins."

"Suppose I bury five gold coins in the field?" said Pinocchio.

"Easy to calculate: Two thousand five hundred shining gold pieces will be yours!"

"Two thousand five hundred! If I shall have two thousand five hundred shining gold pieces, dear friends, you shall have five hundred."

"No, no, no," said the Fox and Cat, "we work only for the good of others."

What good creatures, thought Pinocchio.

And forgetting his papa, his spelling book, and all his good resolutions, he said to the Fox and the Cat: "I will go with you."

THE THREE FRIENDS walked and walked until at last they arrived at the Red Crawfish Inn, where they decided to eat and rest. At midnight they'd start off for the Field of Miracles and arrive at dawn.

But when midnight struck, Pinocchio discovered his companions had left.

"Your good friends said they'd meet you at the Field of Miracles at daybreak," the host said.

Pinocchio paid the host one gold coin and hurried into the darkness. Outside the inn the puppet could not see his hand in front of him it was so pitch dark. Not a leaf moved. When some night birds flying across the road brushed Pinocchio's nose with their wings, he sprang back in terror.

"Who goes there?" he called, quaking, and the surrounding hills echoed, "Who goes there? Who goes there? Who goes there?"

That was when he saw a little insect shining dimly on the trunk of a tree, like a night-light.

"Who are you?" asked Pinocchio.

"I am the ghost of the Talking Cricket. Go back, and take the four gold coins that you have left to your poor father."

"By tomorrow these four coins will have become two thousand."

"Listen to me: go back."

"I will go on."

"The hour is late!"

"I am determined to go on."

"The road is dangerous!"

"I will go on. Good night, Cricket."

"Good night, Pinocchio. May you be saved from dangers and assassins."

No sooner had he said these words than the Talking Cricket vanished like a light that has been blown out, and the dark became darker than ever. Pinocchio began talking to himself.

"I don't believe in assassins, so how can they get me? And if they do exist, which they don't, I shall say to them: 'Gentlemen assassins, remember you are dealing with Pinocchio! So get on with you.'"

He had no sooner finished saying this than he noticed two shadowy figures tiptoeing after him. Assassins! Pinocchio slipped the gold pieces under his tongue and tried to run, but one assassin cried out:

"Your money or your life!"

Pinocchio couldn't speak with the money under his tongue, so he gestured: "I have none."

"Come, come. Deliver it up or you are dead," said the taller of the assassins. "You and your father!"

"No, no, no, not my poor papa!" cried Pinocchio, and with that the gold coins clinked in his mouth.

"Ah, you rascal. You have hidden your money under your tongue."

And one seized the puppet by the nose, the other by the chin, and they tried to pry his mouth open. But Pinocchio bit the one assassin's hand clean off and spat it out. (Imagine his surprise to see he had spat a cat's paw onto the ground!)

Then, using his nails, he freed himself and, jumping the hedge, flew across the countryside, with assassins on his heels like two dogs chasing a hare.

PINOCCHIO RAN AND RAN, when finally and with great relief he saw in the distance amidst dark green trees a small house as white as snow.

"If only I had breath to reach that house, perhaps I could be saved."

He ran again, and at last, breathless, he knocked at the door of the little house.

No one answered. He knocked again—*thunk, thunk, thunk*—for he heard the panting of the assassins behind him. The same silence. Then he kicked and pummeled the door with all his might.

A window opened and a beautiful Child appeared. She had blue hair and a face as white as a statue. Without moving her lips she said:

"In this house there is no one. They are all dead."

"But you are not dead. Oh, beautiful Child with blue hair, open the door." Pinocchio spoke the best he could with the coins in his mouth. "Have compassion on a poor boy pursued by assass—"

At that, he felt himself seized by the collar. "You shall not escape from us again!" a voice said.

The puppet, seeing death staring him in the face, trembled so violently the joints of his wooden legs began to creak, and the coins hidden under his tongue began to clink. Still Pinocchio stubbornly refused to open his mouth, and so the assassins tied his arms behind his back, passed a noose around his throat, and hung him to the branch of the Big Oak Tree.

"Let us hope," one said, "that when we return you will be polite enough to be found quite dead, and with your mouth wide open." Then they walked off.

. . .

A TEMPESTUOUS northerly wind began to blow and roar, and it beat the poor puppet as he hung, making him swing violently like the clatter of a bell.

"Oh, Papa, Papa. If only you were here!" he wailed.

This is what the beautiful Child with blue hair saw when she came to her window: the unhappy Pinocchio hanging, dancing up and down in the gusts of the north wind. She struck her hands together, making three little claps, and a large falcon flew onto the windowsill.

"Your wish, gracious Fairy?" he asked, for it is true the Child with blue hair was no more and no less than a beautiful Fairy, who for more than a thousand years had lived in the wood.

"Fly at once to that puppet dangling from the Big Oak, and bring him to me."

A quarter of an hour later, a carriage brought the poor puppet to the Fairy's door. She carried him into a little room of mother-of-pearl and summoned the most famous doctors: a Crow, an Owl, and a Talking Cricket.

"Gentlemen," she said, "I wish to know if this unfortunate puppet is alive or dead."

Crow felt Pinocchio's pulse, then his nose, then his foot: "In my opinion, the puppet is already quite dead, but if he should not be dead, then it would be a sign that he is alive!"

"I contradict the Crow," said the Owl. "In my opinion, the puppet is still alive, but if, unfortunately, he should not be alive, then it would be a sign that he is dead!"

"And you, you have nothing to say?" the Fairy asked the Talking Cricket.

"In my opinion, the wisest thing a prudent doctor can do, when he doesn't know what he is talking about, is to be silent."

Pinocchio began to tremble.

"But I know that puppet," the Talking Cricket said. "He is a rascal, a ragamuffin, a do-nothing, a vagabond. That puppet is a disobedient son who will make his poor father die of a broken heart!"

At that instant sobs were heard in the room. Imagine everybody's astonishment when they discovered the sounds were coming from Pinocchio.

"When the dead person cries, it is a sign that he is on the road to getting well," said the Crow.

As soon as the three doctors had left the room, the Fairy dissolved some medicine in a glass and offered it to Pinocchio.

"Drink it and you will be better," she said.

"Is it sweet or bitter?"

"Bitter, but it will do you good."

"No, I don't like anything bitter."

"Drink it and I will give you a lump of sugar afterward."

"Give me the lump of sugar first."

The blue Fairy gave him the lump of sugar, but he would not drink the medicine.

"I need another lump of sugar," he said.

The good Fairy, with all the patience of a good mama, put another lump of sugar in his mouth, then presented him the medicine.

"I cannot drink it because that pillow bothers me."

The Fairy removed the pillow.

"I cannot drink it because the door of the room, which is half open, bothers me."

The Fairy closed the door.

"In short, I will not drink the bitter medicine."

That was when Pinocchio saw four rabbits, black as ink, carrying on their shoulders a little coffin. "We have come to take you," they said.

"Oh, Fairy, Fairy, give me the glass of medicine," Pinocchio screamed, and he drank it all up.

SCENE VII

SETTLED BY THE FIREPLACE, the good Fairy asked Pinocchio about the assassins. Pinocchio told her all about Fire-eater, and the gold coins, and the Field of Miracles, and of the hand that was a cat's paw. And of the threat the assassins made that when he was dead, they would come and carry off the pieces of gold that were under his tongue.

"And the gold pieces? Where have you put them?" asked the Fairy.

"I have lost them," said Pinocchio, and his nose grew two fingers longer, for he was telling a lie. He had the coins in his pocket.

"And where did you lose the coins?"

"In the wood near here." His nose grew another two fingers.

"Ah, then we will find them because everything that is lost in that wood is always found."

"No, I remember. I didn't lose the gold pieces; I swallowed them when I was drinking your medicine."

At this third lie, his nose grew to such a length poor

Pinocchio could not move in any direction. The good Fairy looked at him and laughed.

"There are lies that have short legs, and lies that have long noses. Your lie, Pinocchio, is one that has a long nose."

Not knowing where to hide, Pinocchio tried to run out of the room, but his nose was so long he could no longer pass through the door.

What was Pinocchio to do there in the doorway! The Fairy let him cry, but only for a while. Then she beat her hands together, and at that, a thousand woodpeckers flew in the window and pecked Pinocchio's nose right down to size.

"What a good Fairy you are," said the puppet, "and how much I love you!"

"I love you also," answered the Fairy, "and if you will remain with me, you shall be my little brother and I will be your good little sister."

"But my poor papa . . ."

"He will be here tonight."

Pinocchio jumped for joy. "I shall go and meet him," he cried.

THAT IS EXACTLY what Pinocchio did, but along the way, almost in front of the Big Oak, who should he meet but the Fox and the Cat. He told them how he had met the dreadful assassins who wanted to rob him.

"Villains!" said the Fox.

"Infamous villains!" repeated the Cat, who Pinocchio noticed had somehow lost her paw.

Pinocchio showed them the very Oak Tree where the assassins had hung him.

"Where can respectable people like us find a haven!" Fox said. ". . . And your gold pieces?"

"I have them in my pocket," said Pinocchio, proudly.

"To think those four gold pieces might still become two thousand by tomorrow. . . . Won't you bury them in the Field of Miracles, my friend?"

"No, no, not today. My papa is coming."

"It will only take a few minutes to collect two thousand gold coins. . . ." said the Fox.

Pinocchio thought of the good Fairy, old Geppetto, and the Talking Cricket, but the field was only a few miles away, and so in the end he went with the Fox and the Cat, who left him at the miracle tree.

There, Pinocchio dug a hole and put in the four gold pieces. Then he filled up the hole with a little earth, took two pails of water from the canal, sprinkled it along with two pinches of salt, and slept in a nearby woods.

When Pinocchio returned to the tree in the morning, his heart beating *tic, tac, tic, tac* like a clock on the wall, he dreamed of branches of gold, and of the beautiful palace it would buy, and of wooden horses and rooms full of candies and tarts.

But when he arrived, there was no gold-coin tree. Pinocchio dug and dug, and dug, but the money was no longer there. He rushed to town and told a judge of the two knaves who had robbed him. Oh, the judge listened, was touched, was moved. Then he rang a bell, and when the guards appeared, said:

"This poor devil has been robbed of four gold pieces; put him immediately into prison."

POOR PINOCCHIO. For four months—four long months—the little puppet remained locked up. You can imagine how quickly he went to the Fairy's house when he was finally released.

"Will the Fairy forgive me?" he said to himself. "Will my papa be at the Fairy's house? It has been so long since I saw him."

But when he arrived at the wood where the little house should have been, it was nowhere to be seen.

28

There was instead a marble stone on which were engraved these sad words:

HERE LIES
the CHILD WITH the BLUE HAIR
WHO DIED FROM SORROW
BECAUSE SHE WAS ABANDONED BY HER
LITTLE BROTHER PINOCCHIO

Pinocchio burst into tears and covered the tombstone with a thousand kisses.

"Oh, little Fairy," he wept, "why did you die? And where can my papa be? Oh, little Fairy, if you really love your little brother, come to life again."

Just then a large Pigeon flew overhead, and called down to him,

"What are you doing there?"

"I am crying!" said Pinocchio.

"Tell me, do you know a puppet called Pinocchio?"

"Pinocchio? I am Pinocchio!"

The Pigeon flew to the ground. She was larger than a turkey.

"Do you also know Geppetto?" she asked.

"Do I know him! He is my poor papa! Is he still alive?"

"I left him only three days ago on the seashore, building a little boat to cross the ocean. He has taken it into his head to go across the world in search of you."

"What a fine thing it would be to have wings!"

"If you wish to go to him, I will carry you."

"How?"

"Astride my back."

With that Pinocchio jumped at once onto the Pigeon's back, and exclaimed, "Gallop, gallop, my little horse, for I am anxious to see my papa!"

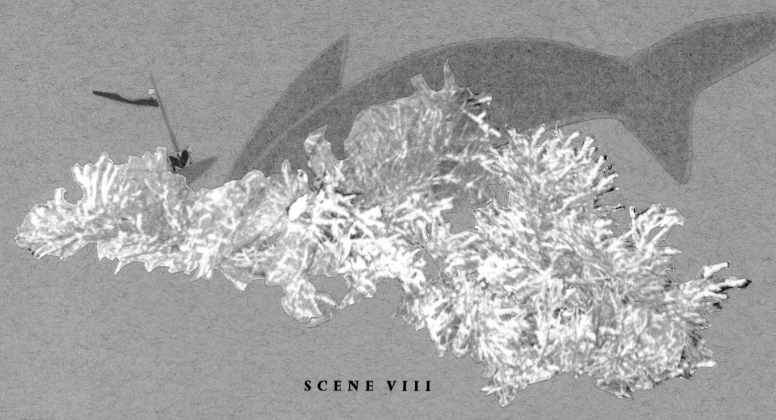

SCENE VIII

WHEN THE PIGEON set him down, Pinocchio saw a great crowd of people watching a boat in a stormy sea. It was in danger of sinking.

Suddenly Pinocchio cried: "It is my papa!"

And when a great wave rose and the boat disappeared, Pinocchio jumped from a rock into the sea.

"I will save my papa!" he said.

The poor boy swam the whole night. Rain fell and he swam. Thunder rolled and he swam. Finally he saw an island, but could not reach it because of the waves. At last one billowed up and threw him onto the sand. He was completely alone. But he saw a fish swimming by.

"Sir Fish," he said. "Have you by chance met a little boat with my papa in it?"

"During the terrible storm, the little boat must have gone to the bottom."

"And my papa?"

"He must have been swallowed by the terrible Dog-fish, who has been swimming in these waters lately. He is bigger than a five-story house, and his mouth is so deep a railway train with a smoking engine could pass down it."

Pinocchio started walking so fast he was nearly running. He only turned now and then to see if the monster fish were following him! Finally he reached a village, where everyone was working. Busy as bees! That was not for him, but he saw a woman carrying two cans of water.

"May I have some?" he said to the woman.

"Drink, my boy," said the little woman. Pinocchio drank like a fish.

"Now if I could only have a little to eat."

"If you will help me carry home these two cans of water, I will give you a piece of bread."

Pinocchio looked at the cans.

"And a nice dish of cauliflower with oil and vinegar . . ." the little woman went on.

Pinocchio answered neither yes nor no.

"And after the cauliflower a bonbon full of syrup."

That temptation Pinocchio could not resist. "I will carry your water can to the house."

When he reached the house, Pinocchio sat down at a small table already laid, and ate everything on the table. When he raised his head to thank the woman, he gave a long "Ohhhhhhh."

"What is it?" said the woman, laughing.

"It is . . ." he said, "you are like . . . the same voice . . . the same hair . . . yes, yes, yes, you also have blue hair. Oh, little Fairy, it is you, really you."

And throwing himself at her feet, he embraced her knees and began to cry.

This time, the blue Fairy not only agreed to be his mama. "Dear Pinocchio," she said, "if you will be a good little puppet, I promise that you will become a real boy. But you must obey me and do everything that I bid you."

"Willingly, willingly, willingly," Pinocchio shouted, jumping for joy. That was what he wanted to be—a real little boy!

"Then tomorrow you will begin school."

Pinocchio became at once a little less joyful.

"It is too late for me to go to school," he said in a low voice.

"It is never too late."

"But it will tire me to go to school."

"Pinocchio!"

"Yes, yes, yes. I am tired of being a puppet. I wish at any price to become a boy."

"Now, it depends on you."

The following day Pinocchio went to school. Imagine the delight of all the real little boys to see a puppet in school. One carried off his cap, another pulled his jacket, still another attempted to tie strings to his feet and hands to make him dance.

Pinocchio stuck his leg out from under the table and gave the last boy a great kick in his shins.

"Oh, what hard feet!" he roared.

Then Pinocchio gave another a blow in the stomach. From that moment on the schoolboys respected Pinocchio, and Pinocchio did all of his work, just as he had promised. Indeed, he kept his word for the season. The entire season.

One day the Fairy said to him, "Tomorrow your wish shall be granted."

"And that is?"

"Tomorrow you shall cease to be a wooden puppet. You shall become a real boy."

A breakfast party was prepared, the likes of which no one on the island had ever heard of before. All his school fellows were invited. Two hundred cups of coffee and milk and four hundred rolls cut and buttered were prepared. What could possibly spoil this wonderful affair?

Nothing! And so, Pinocchio wanted to go around the town to deliver his own invitations.

The Fairy said to him: "Go if you like, my Pinocchio, but return before dark."

"I shall be back in an hour," answered the puppet.

"Children are very ready to promise. It is what they do that I am interested in."

"I am not like other children; I keep my word."

"We shall see, Pinocchio," the blue Fairy said.

In less than an hour all his friends were invited. And once they heard there would be rolls and coffee, they agreed to come. All except one. Pinocchio's favorite: Candlewick.

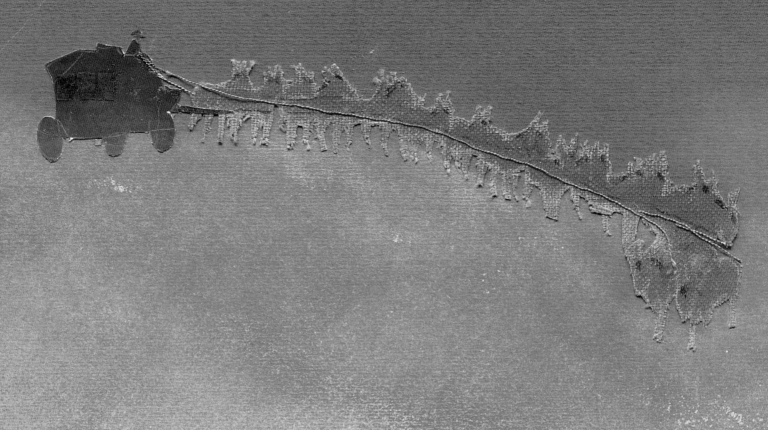

SCENE IX

CANDLEWICK WAS the laziest and naughtiest boy in the entire school, but Pinocchio was devoted to him. Pinocchio had gone once, twice, three times to his cottage, but he was not there. He looked here and there. At last he saw Candlewick hiding on the porch of a peasant's cottage.

"What are you doing there?" asked Pinocchio.

"I am waiting for dark. . . ."

"Why? Where are you going?"

"I am going very far, very far, very far away."

"But haven't you heard? Tomorrow I become a boy like you! You must come to my breakfast party."

"But I am going away tonight."

"Where?"

"To the most delightful country in the world: the Land of Toys. Come with me, Pinocchio."

"Me? Never."

"Listen. Where would you find a better place to be? There are no schools, no masters, no books, no studies—because on Thursday there is never school, and every week consists of six Thursdays and one Sunday."

"But what do you do there?"

"Play from morning until night!"

"Hmmmm," said Pinocchio.

"Will you come?"

"No. No, no, and again no. I promised my blue Fairy to become a good boy. I will keep my word. Goodbye, Candlewick."

"Wait two minutes."

"No, it will make me late. . . . Are you going to make this trip alone?"

32

"No, there will be a hundred boys."

"Will you make the journey on foot?"

"A coach will pass by here and collect me. Stay just another two minutes and you will see."

"Well, just two minutes . . ."

There had been so much talking that night had crept in, and it was already quite dark. Suddenly they saw in the distance a small light moving, and they heard a buzz of talking and the sound of a trumpet, but so small and feeble that it sounded like the hum of a mosquito.

"Here it is!" shouted Candlewick, jumping to his feet. "It is the coach coming to take me. Now will you come? Yes or no."

Now, the most extraordinary thing about this coach was that it was pulled by twelve pairs of donkeys of all different colors. Some gray, some white, some brindled like pepper and salt. And instead of being shod like other beasts, on their feet they wore laced shoes made of leather.

And the coachman? Picture a little man broader than he was long, flabby and greasy like a lump of butter, with a small round face like an orange, a little mouth that was always laughing, and a soft, caressing voice like a cat.

The coach was full of boys between eight and twelve years old, heaped one upon another like herrings in a barrel. All of the boys wanted to sit next to the coachman. Indeed, since there was no place in the coach at all, Candlewick gave a leap and sat himself on the springs!

"Come with us, Pinocchio!" shouted Candlewick. "We shall have such fun!"

"Come with us," shouted the hundred boys.

Pinocchio sighed and sighed, and then sighed for a third time, and finally said, "Make room for me, I am coming too!"

Pinocchio leaped onto one of the donkeys, but as it galloped down the road he thought he heard a low voice say to him: "Poor fool! You would follow your own way, but you will be sorry."

Pinocchio looked from side to side, but could see nobody.

Then he heard the same voice say, "A day will come when you will weep, but then it will be too late! Too late, too late."

THE LAND OF TOYS was an amazing country. Boys were everywhere, playing. Some were playing ball, some rode bicycles, others wooden horses. Some played hide-and-seek. Some were singing, some leaping, some walking on their hands with their feet in the air; others strutted about dressed as generals. Some were laughing, some shouting, some whistling. Such pandemonium! Such an uproar of voices! And theaters everywhere with inscriptions on the walls:

LONG LIVE TOYS!

DOWN WITH ARITHMETIC

NO MORE SCHOOLS

And so on. And so on.

Pinocchio, Candlewick, and the other boys had no sooner set foot in the town when they began to join the fun. How could they be happier!

And in the midst of continual games and amusement, the hours, days, and weeks passed like lightning.

"What a wonderful life!" Pinocchio said, whenever by chance he met Candlewick. "And I have you to thank for it."

THIS LIFE HAD GONE ON for five months, when one morning Pinocchio awoke to a most unpleasant surprise. What was it? Pinocchio awoke, scratched his head, and discovered that his ears had grown. He went at once in search of a mirror, but found a basin of water instead. There he saw that his ears, broomish ears, had grown into a magnificent pair of donkey's ears.

Oh, the shame!

He began to cry and roar, but the more he cried and roared the longer the ears grew. And grew and grew. It was a dormouse who popped up out of the floor and announced to Pinocchio that he had a fever!

"What fever?" said Pinocchio.

"Donkey fever," said the dormouse. "And in two or three hours you will be no longer a puppet, or a boy . . . you will become really and truly a little donkey!"

Pinocchio tried to pull his donkey ears off.

"All boys who are lazy and pass all their days with toys and games end up by becoming little donkeys!"

"The fault is all Candlewick's!" Pinocchio wailed. "He's the one who told me not to bother with school. He's the one who asked me to come along to the Land of Toys!"

"Are you not the one who followed the bad advice?"

"Yes! Because I am a puppet with no sense. And with no heart!"

Suddenly Pinocchio was determined to find Candlewick. Ashamed of his ears, he pulled a big cotton bag down over them and searched for Candlewick—in the streets, the squares, the little theaters. But he could not find him.

Finally he went to his house, where he discovered Candlewick—with a bag on his head, just like his own!

"Oh, poor Candlewick!"

"Oh, poor Pinocchio! Can we have the same illness?"

"I am afraid so. Will you do me a kindness, Candlewick?"

"Willingly! With all my heart."

"Will you let me see your ears?"

"Why not? But first, my dear Pinocchio, I should like to see yours."

"I know, we should both take our bags off at the same moment!"

"I agree."

"Then, one, two, three!"

At the word three, the two boys took off the bags and threw them into the air. When the two discovered their misfortune, instead of grieving, they began to laugh. They laughed and laughed and laughed.

But all of a sudden Candlewick stopped, staggered, and, changing color, said to his friend:

"Help, help, Pinocchio!"

"What is the matter with you?"

"I cannot stand up."

"Nor can I," said Pinocchio, tottering.

And while they were talking, they both doubled up and began to run around the room on their hands and feet. As they ran, their hands became hooves, their faces lengthened into muzzles, their backs became covered with long gray hairs, and instead of sighing they brayed like donkeys: *He-ja, he-ja, he-ja!*

It was at that moment the coachman came in and led the two little donkeys off to the marketplace, where

Candlewick was bought by a peasant, and Pinocchio was sold to a circus director. (And now you know the truth about the coachman!)

POOR PINOCCHIO. Led to his new master, he was put into a stall and given nothing but hay. Since there was nothing else, he chewed a little and swallowed it. It wasn't new bread and a fine slice of sausage, but it was something.

In the morning his new master woke him: "Up, then, at once," he said. "I will teach you to jump through hoops, through flaming frames of paper, to dance waltzes and polkas, and to stand upright on your hind legs."

Poor Pinocchio had to learn all of these things. But it took him three months and as many whippings before he learned them all.

Finally his master put up a sign:

TONIGHT
THE FAMOUS
LITTLE DONKEY
PINOCCHIO
THE STAR OF THE DANCE
WILL MAKE HIS FIRST
APPEARANCE

That night the theater was overflowing with boys and girls of all ages. The ringmaster, dressed in a red coat, gray pants, and big leather boots, came out to a theater crammed with people.

After making a deep bow, he began:

"From the courts of the Emperor of all of Europe, a celebrated little donkey. Not an easy animal to tame. Found in the wilds of Africa, he was a savage beast. Notice the wild rolling of his eyes. But here is my discovery: See this bump? This bump gives him an extraordinary talent for dancing. You can judge how great!"

Then the ringmaster made another deep bow, and turned to Pinocchio.

"Courage, Pinocchio! Before you begin your feats, make your bow to this distinguished audience—ladies, gentlemen, and children."

Pinocchio obeyed, and bent both his knees till they touched the ground. Then the ringmaster cracked the whip.

"Walk!"

The little donkey walked.

"Trot!" the ringmaster cried.

Pinocchio obeyed.

"Gallop!"

Pinocchio broke into a gallop.

"Full gallop!"

Pinocchio went full gallop.

Then, while Pinocchio was going full speed, the ringmaster raised his arm and fired off a pistol. The little donkey fell, pretending to have been wounded. When he got up from the ground, amid cheers and clapping of hands, he raised his head. There in one of the boxes he saw a beautiful lady who wore around her neck a thick gold chain from which hung a locket. On the medallion was painted the portrait of a puppet.

SCENE XI

THAT IS MY PORTRAIT. . . . That beautiful lady is my Fairy," said Pinocchio, and he began to cry, "Oh, my little Fairy, oh, my little Fairy."

But instead of these words a bray came from him, so loud the spectators laughed. Especially the children.

The ringmaster gave him a blow on his nose for making such noise.

"Now let the audience see how gracefully you can jump through the hoop," the ringmaster said.

Pinocchio tried two or three times, but each time he went over it or under it. At last he made a leap and went through it, but his right leg caught in the hoop and he fell.

The ringmaster pulled Pinocchio offstage. Though the audience cheered, "Bring out Pinocchio! Bring out Pinocchio!" the little donkey was seen no more. The ringmaster had no use for a lame donkey, and the next day he sold him to a stable boy who intended to use

his skin for a drum. Imagine how Pinocchio felt at hearing he would become a drum!

But that is exactly what the stable boy planned, so he took Pinocchio to a high cliff overlooking the sea to push him off the edge and drown him first. When the boy began to put the rope around the donkey's feet, Pinocchio gave him a kick and dived into the sea.

It was when he was at the bottom of the sea that his hooves became feet, the long gray hairs turned into skin, and his ears became the ears of a puppet again. Now, the little puppet swam to the top, and swam and swam, until he saw a large rock in the middle of the sea! On it stood a little Goat bleating and calling out to the puppet to come to her.

There was something strange about that little Goat. Her coat was not white or black or brown like other goats, but azure blue. The deep blue of the hair of his Fairy.

SCENE XII

PINOCCHIO'S HEART beat fast, then faster and faster as he swam toward the white rock. He was almost halfway there when a horrible sea monster stuck its head out of the water. It was the enormous Dogfish that everyone had spoken of.

Poor Pinocchio! He tried to swim away from the Dogfish, to change his path, to escape, but that giant mouth with its three rows of gleaming white teeth kept coming nearer and nearer.

"Come here, Pinocchio, I beg you," bleated the little Goat on the high rock.

Pinocchio swam desperately toward her, with his arms, his body, his legs, his feet.

"Faster, Pinocchio. Quick, quick, or you are lost!"

Pinocchio reached the rock, and the Goat leaned over to give him one of her hooves when, alas! he found himself between the rows of gleaming white teeth.

The Dogfish took an immense *gulp!* and swallowed the little puppet. Down, down he fell. When he recovered, he was surrounded by darkness, a darkness so deep and so black he thought he had put his head into an inkwell.

"Help! Help!" Pinocchio cried. "Won't someone come to save me?"

But there was only the darkness, and the occasional cold wind. Then, in the distance, the puppet saw a faint light. Tottering in the darkness, he walked toward the light, his feet splashing in the slippery water.

On and on he walked, the light growing brighter and clearer, when finally he found—I will give you a thousand guesses what, my young friends—he found a little table set for dinner and lighted by a candle stuck in a glass bottle. Near the table sat a little old man, white as snow, eating live fish.

The little puppet wanted to laugh, he wanted to cry, he wanted to say a thousand things, but all he could do was to stand there, stuttering and stammering. At last he let out a scream of joy, and opening wide his arms, he threw them around the old man's neck.

"Father," he cried, "dear Father, I have found you at last."

"Pinocchio! Pinocchio!"

"How long have you been here?"

"Two long, weary years, Pinocchio."

"But where did you get the candle? And the matches to light it?"

"In the very storm which swamped my boat, a large ship suffered the same fate. The terrible Dogfish swallowed most of it."

40

"Swallowed a ship?" asked Pinocchio in astonishment.

"At one gulp. The only thing he spat out was the mainmast. The ship was loaded with meat, crackers, bread, bottles of wine, raisins, cheese, boxes of matches, and wax candles, though this is the last candle you see here."

"And then?"

"And then, my dear, we will find ourselves in darkness."

"Then, my dear father," said Pinocchio, "there is no time to lose. We must try to escape."

"But how?"

"We can run out of the monster's mouth, and dive into the sea!"

"But, my dear Pinocchio, I cannot swim."

"I am a fine swimmer. You will climb on my shoulders, and I will carry you safely to the shore."

"Dreams, my boy," answered Geppetto. "Do you think it possible for a puppet, a yard high, to carry an old man on his shoulders—and swim?"

"We will try it and see."

And without adding another word, Pinocchio took the candle in his hand and led his father down the long, dark throat of the giant fish.

WHAT THE PUPPET and the old man discovered was that the Dogfish, being very old and suffering from asthma, slept with his mouth open. Pinocchio could even catch a glimpse of the star-filled sky as he looked through the open jaws. And so they climbed, softly, up the throat of the monster till they came to that immense, open mouth.

And the two were about to dive into the sea when the Dogfish sneezed, so suddenly, Pinocchio and Geppetto were jolted back into the stomach of the monster.

The candle went out.

"Now we are lost," Geppetto said sadly.

"Why lost? Give me your hand, dear Father. We must try again."

With these words Pinocchio took his father by the hand, and on tiptoes they climbed up the monster's throat for a second time. This time they crossed the whole tongue and jumped over three rows of teeth.

"Now, climb on my back and hold onto my neck."

As soon as Geppetto was comfortably seated on his shoulders, Pinocchio dived into the water and started to swim. The sea was like oil, the moon shone, and the Dogfish continued to sleep so soundly that not even a cannon shot would have awakened him.

Pinocchio swam toward land as swiftly as he could,

but it was a long way away. When the little puppet finally touched land, Pinocchio offered his arm to Geppetto, who could hardly stand.

"Let's go, Father."

PINOCCHIO and his father had not taken a hundred steps when they saw two rough-looking shadows sitting on a stone, begging. It was the Fox and the Cat. The Cat, pretending to be blind for so many years, had really lost her sight. And the Fox, old and thin, had lost his tail. He had been forced to sell it for a bite to eat.

"Please, Pinocchio, give us some alms."

"False friends," answered the puppet. "You cheated me once, twice, but you will never cheat me again."

"Believe us! We are truly poor and starving."

"If you are poor, you deserve it! Remember the proverb 'Stolen money never bears fruit.' "

"Have mercy . . ." said the Fox.

"On us," said the Cat.

"Remember the old proverb that says 'Bad wheat always makes poor bread!' "

"Do not abandon us!"

"Remember the old proverb that says 'Whoever steals his neighbor's shirt dies without his own.' "

Waving goodbye to them, Pinocchio and Geppetto calmly went their way. When they came to a tiny cottage built of straw, Pinocchio knocked at the door.

"Who is it?" said a little voice from within.

"A poor father and a poorer son without food and with no roof for cover," answered Pinocchio.

"Turn the key," said the same little voice.

When Pinocchio entered the cottage he saw no one.

"Here I am, up here!"

Pinocchio looked up at the ceiling, and there on a beam sat the Talking Cricket.

"Dear Cricket!" Pinocchio said.

"How can you call me 'dear Cricket'? You threw a hammer at me."

"You are right, you are right. At least spare my poor father."

"I am going to spare both father and son. I have only wanted you to know that in this world of ours, if we want kindness and courtesy, we must be kind to others. And courteous, too."

"And this cottage?"

"A little Goat with blue hair gave it to me."

"But where did the little Goat go?"

"She will not be back. She went bleating sadly, 'Poor Pinocchio, I shall never see him again.'"

Pinocchio began to cry. "The Goat was the dear little blue Fairy."

Then he made a bed of straw for Geppetto, and went to get a glass of milk from the farmer down the lane. When the farmer said a full glass would cost a penny, Pinocchio said he had none. When the farmer said he could have a glass for pulling water from a well, Pinocchio said he'd try.

And that is what Pinocchio did. Before long, he had pulled up one hundred buckets. He had never worked so hard in his life.

"Until today," said the farmer, "my Donkey had drawn the water for me, but now that poor animal is dying."

"Will you take me to see him?" said Pinocchio.

As soon as Pinocchio went into the stable, he spied a little Donkey lying on a bed of straw. He was worn out from hunger and too much work.

Pinocchio bent over to look closely. "I think I know that Donkey!" he said. "It is, it is . . ."

"Yes . . . Candlewick," the Donkey said softly, then he closed his eyes and died.

"Oh, my poor Candlewick," said Pinocchio.

Every day for the next five months Pinocchio got up in the morning just as dawn was breaking and went to the farm to draw water. And every day he was given a glass of warm milk for his poor old father, who grew stronger and better day by day. Before long he began to make baskets each night after supper to sell. Eight each night.

One day, when he had saved fifty pennies, he said to his father: "I am going to the marketplace to buy myself a coat, a cap, and a pair of shoes."

But when he ran out of the house and up the road to the village, laughing and singing, he met a large snail crawling out of some bushes. She told Pinocchio that the blue Fairy was not gone but very, very ill.

He gave the snail all his pennies to help the blue Fairy, and that night instead of going to bed at ten, he worked until midnight. If he had helped his papa, he could help his Fairy. And instead of making eight baskets, he made sixteen.

He dreamed that night of his Fairy, who smiled and said, "Bravo, Pinocchio. In reward for your kind heart, you will have a good and happy life."

At that moment Pinocchio awoke and opened his eyes. He looked all about him. Instead of the usual walls of straw, he found himself in a beautifully furnished little room. He jumped from his bed to look on the chair standing nearby. There he found a new suit, new hat, and a pair of shoes.

Pinocchio ran to the mirror. He hardly recognized himself. The bright face of a real boy looked at him with wide-awake blue eyes, dark brown hair, and happy, smiling lips.

"And where is Father?" he suddenly cried.

He ran into the next room, and there stood Geppetto, grown years younger overnight, spick and span in new clothes, once more Mastro Geppetto, the wood-carver. He was hard at work on a lovely picture frame, decorating it with flowers and leaves and heads of animals.

"Father, Father, what has happened?" cried Pinocchio.

"When people become good, they have more power than they can imagine!"

"And old Pinocchio?"

"There he is." Leaning against a chair was a large wooden puppet, head turned to one side, arms hanging limp, and legs twisted under him.

"How ridiculous I was as a puppet! And how happy I am now that I am a real boy!"

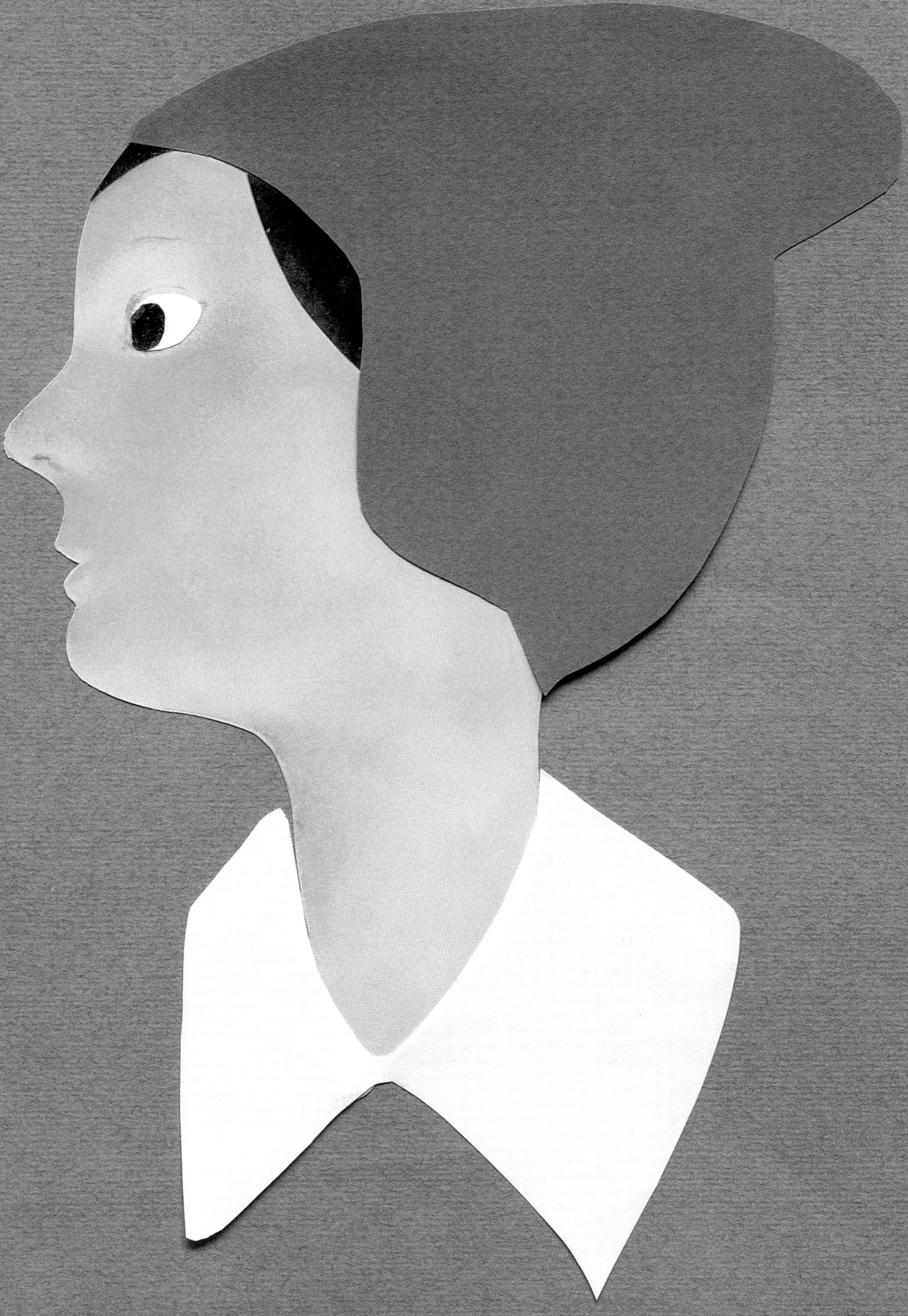